Shiva

Subhadra Sen Gupta has written over thirty books for children. Right now she is waiting for a time machine so that she can travel to the past and join Emperor Akbar for lunch. She loves to travel, flirt with cats and chat with autorickshaw drivers. If you want to discuss anything under the sun with her, email her at subhadrasg@gmail.com

Tapas Guha has been working for more than twenty years as an illustrator. He loves to draw comics and illustrate children's books. Ruskin Bond is one of his favourite authors and he loves Tintin comics.

Shiva

SUBHADRA SEN GUPTA

Illustrated by
TAPAS GUHA

RED TURTLE
RUPA

Published in Red Turtle by
Rupa Publications India Pvt. Ltd 2017
7/16, Ansari Road, Daryaganj
New Delhi 110002

Sales centres:
Allahabad Bengaluru Chennai
Hyderabad Jaipur Kathmandu
Kolkata Mumbai

ISBN: 978-81-291-4514-7

First impression 2017

10 9 8 7 6 5 4 3 2 1

CONTENTS

A River Lands on Shiva's Head

A long, long time ago, there was a beautiful river goddess named Ganga. She flowed through Swarga, the home of all gods and goddesses. Her silvery blue water rippled past fields carpeted with green grass and brightly coloured flowers. Butterflies flitted about and bees hummed

as they sipped on delicious nectar.

Swarga was a happy, peaceful place. Apsaras, the beautiful dancers of heaven, bathed in Ganga's crystal waterfalls as she frothed over rocks and cliffs, while musicians called gandharvas sat by her banks and sang to her. Ganga loved being the river of heaven.

Meanwhile, exciting things were happening on earth. Sagara, the powerful king of Ayodhya, had a huge army that no one could defeat. One day, Sagara decided to perform a very special ceremony, a horse sacrifice called the ashvamedha yagna. He prayed to the gods to make his kingdom bigger and stronger. Then a handsome white stallion wearing the royal pennant was set free to roam wherever it wanted.

When the horse entered another kingdom, its king had a choice—he could bow before the horse and accept Sagara as his king, or he could fight Sagara's army. As you can guess, the ashvamedha yagna was a very clever way to conquer other kingdoms, because most kings would rather pay tribute to mighty monarchs such as Sagara than fight against them!

Soon, tributes came pouring into Ayodhya from the lands around. The city was filled with precious jewels, gold, silver, bolts of silk and logs of sandalwood. As his horse wandered about the countryside, Sagara's kingdom grew and grew and he also became very rich.

The gods were watching the events on earth. Among them was Lord Indra, who was the king of Swarga. Being a famous warrior, he was also the commander-in-chief of the army of the gods. As Sagara's armies marched through one kingdom after another, Indra began to feel jealous. 'This is terrible!'

he thought. 'I am the mightiest general of all. I have defeated thousands of demons and won hundreds of battles. I cannot allow this earthly king to rival my power. But what can I do to stop Sagara?'

Indra thought up a cunning plan. One moonless night, he came down to earth, unnoticed in the dark, and stole Sagara's white horse. He led it away to the hermitage of a sage named Rishi Kapila. This sage lived in a thatched hut in a forest by the sea and spent his time in meditation, which meant that he would sit for days with his eyes closed, concentrating on his prayers. The sage did not see Indra hiding the horse in the trees near his hut.

Next morning, Sagara's soldiers woke up to discover that the white stallion had vanished! There was utter panic in the army camp. Men were sent off to search in every direction but no one could find the horse. Finally, the army commander had to tell Sagara the news. As he spoke, King Sagara's eyes grew alarmingly round and red with anger.

'How could you lose a horse?' he yelled.

'We've looked everywhere, Your Majesty.' The commander hung his head in shame. 'We've searched in the hills and the valleys, the forests, the fields, the towns and the villages...'

Sagara turned to his chief minister. 'Call my sons. They are clever boys. They'll know what to do.'

Now, it is written in the ancient books that Sagara had 60,000 sons! This is rather hard to believe. Perhaps the storytellers of old were only trying to make their tales more exciting, but it is possible that Sagara did have a lot of sons, enough to make up a huge search party. They set out to find the missing white stallion. Only one son, whose name was Asamanjas, stayed back in Ayodhya.

The sons of Sagara went deep into the forest. They climbed mountains. They trudged through deserts. They peered into caves. Then, in desperation, they began to search underground for the horse. They dug and they dug, and they dug so deep that they created an ocean. Finally, at long last, they discovered the horse frolicking on the sands by the edge of this ocean.

'How ever did it get here?' they wondered. 'The horse could never have travelled so far from the army and our kingdom.'

‘I think he must have stolen it,’ said one of Sagara’s sons, pointing to Rishi Kapila who was, as always, meditating silently in his hut.

Now, Sagara’s sons were not well-mannered boys and they thought that being very rich princes gave them the right to do anything they wanted. They surrounded old Rishi Kapila and shouted insults at him, even calling him a horse thief!

Rishis are usually peace-loving people, but when they lose their temper, oh boy! They become really dangerous. Kapila did not like being disturbed during his prayers and being called a thief made him very angry. He opened his eyes and cursed the princes. When they replied rudely, fire poured out of the sage’s eyes and Sagara’s sons were instantly burnt to ashes. Calm and quiet returned to his forest, and Kapila closed his eyes again in meditation, as the ashes of Sagara’s dead sons lay in a forgotten heap on the sand.

When Sagara heard what had happened, he was filled with grief for his dead sons. And then he was told that Kapila’s curses meant that the souls of the boys would

never reach heaven. Sagara's heart almost broke at the thought. He hurried to the hermitage to beg the sage's forgiveness and ask for his help. Rishi Kapila said that once he had pronounced a curse it could not be taken back and only Ganga could save the boys' souls. He suggested that Sagara should pray to the river goddess to come down to earth and wash away the ashes with her divine waters. The souls of Sagara's sons would then surely reach heaven.

Sagara prayed long and hard to Ganga, but the goddess wanted to remain in heaven

and refused to flow down to earth. The poor king died while trying to coax her into changing her mind. Then his son Asamanjas, his grandson Anshuman and his great-grandson Dilip all spent their lives trying to persuade Ganga to bring her waters to the earth, but she ignored their prayers.

Finally, Sagara's great-great-grandson Bhagirath decided to give it one last try. He was a very determined man, and he went to snowy Kedarnath, high up amongst the mountains of the Himalayas, and prayed and prayed. He hardly ate, seldom slept and kept on praying till Ganga, driven crazy by his constant pleas, finally agreed to wash away the ashes.

Now here arose another problem! Ganga was very reluctant to leave her heavenly home, and so, when the river turned towards earth, she flowed down in an angry, fierce torrent. Brahma, the lord of creation who had made the heavens and the earth, watched in horror as the tumultuous waters began to smash through mountains and rocks, flooding homes and fields. Brahma ran towards Lord Shiva's home on Mount Kailash where he lived with his wife Parvati.

Brahma cried out, 'Oh Shiva, my friend, you must help me! My world is about to be destroyed by this bad-tempered goddess.'

Shiva was surprised. 'But Brahma, what can I do? If Ganga does not listen to you, she will never obey me,' he said.

Parvati laughed. 'I am his wife and even I don't always obey him.'

But Brahma was desperate. 'Do something, please!'

he pleaded. At the same time, Bhagirath also began to pray to Shiva, and Shiva is a god who never refuses to help.

Shiva sat cross-legged under a tree, closed his eyes and meditated. Then, as Parvati and Brahma watched in wonder, Shiva's body began to grow until he was bigger than the mountains and his head touched the sky. This giant god then strode across the Himalayas and reached the spot where Ganga was cascading down a hill. He calmly placed himself beneath the torrent of water and it crashed on to his head.

Shiva, you may have noticed, has an interesting hairstyle. It is all knotted and coiled on top of his head, and as Ganga flowed through the complicated twists and curls, she got quite lost. She flowed slower and slower, and eventually had to beg Shiva to set her free. Shiva broke her up into seven gentle streams before he allowed her out of his hair. These

seven streams flowed down from the high mountains. Six of them met just before the city of Haridwar and merged their waters again into the great river we call Ganga. Yamuna, the seventh stream, joined Ganga at Allahabad.

By now the goddess had calmed down. She was no longer in a temper, and Bhagirath could walk before her, guiding her to the ocean, all the way across the flat lands of northern India. At last they reached the sandy shores of the Bay of Bengal where the ashes of Sagara's sons still lay. The cool river water flowed over the ashes so that their souls could finally reach heaven. Then Ganga, her work done and tired after her long journey, flowed into the ocean.

So now you know why Shiva always has a river rising like a fountain from his topknot. Every day, millions of worshippers offer water to this god with the strange hairdo, to thank him for bringing us Ganga, the mighty river who makes crops grow, provides drinking water and also helps souls make their journey to heaven. The spot where Sagara's sons were burnt to ashes by Rishi Kapila is now the sandy island of Ganga Sagar.

Shiva Becomes A Glittering Pillar

Sometimes Shiva, the lord of destruction, is shown as the dancer Nataraj. At other times he sits cross-legged in meditation as Mahadev. But strangest of all, there are times when he is represented in temples as just a column of black stone, a shivalingam. Other Hindu deities appear as handsome warriors, and our goddesses are clad in expensive silk and jewels. So why does Shiva take the shape of a plain stone column?

It all began with an argument between the three greatest Hindu gods—Brahma, Vishnu and Shiva. They are the Great Trinity responsible for the three worlds—the heavens called Swarga, the earth called Prithvi and the netherworld called Pataal. Brahma creates them, Vishnu preserves them and Shiva destroys them so that the cycle of creation can start again. When it is time for the worlds to end, especially when evil seems to be taking over, Shiva begins to dance the tandava dance and everything burns and turns to ashes under his dancing feet.

Now, one day, the three gods were sitting together in Swarga when Vishnu wondered aloud, 'Here we are, the most powerful of all the gods, but who is the greatest of us three?'

Brahma's five heads nodded wisely. 'I am the greatest, of course. I create the three worlds and I am also the oldest—see my white hair and beard? So you two must worship me.'

Vishnu laughed. He is a handsome, dark-skinned god, who dresses like a king in cloths of gold and sparkling jewellery. 'I disagree,' he said. 'What would you do without me, Lord Brahma? You create the three worlds and then close your eyes and go back to your meditation. If I did not take care of your creations, they would all fall apart. The gods and goddesses in Swarga would be unhappy and people on earth would starve and die. I am the one who keeps the worlds working properly.'

Shiva had been listening silently to this

conversation as he sat cross-legged on his tiger skin. Now he said, 'But the whole cycle of creation would stop if I didn't destroy everything. Brahma would not be able to create and you, Vishnu, would be trying to preserve old and dying worlds. I am, naturally, the greatest.'

Their argument became quite heated until Vishnu said, 'We have to ask someone to solve this mystery. Why don't we ask the Vedas? They are the four books of wisdom, the oldest books, and they know everything.'

The Vedas were summoned and all four said together, 'Lord Shiva is the greatest! He not only destroys but can also create and preserve. Only he can do all three jobs. He is Mahadev, the greatest of the gods.'

Shiva smiled happily. 'Aha!' he thought. 'These two headstrong friends of mine will now have to bow before me. After all, the Vedas know best.'

But Brahma and Vishnu looked at each other in dismay. Worship Shiva? Never! And they began to walk away.

Now Shiva can be kind and patient but he also

has a very bad temper. When he saw Brahma and Vishnu turning their backs on him, he exploded in anger. 'You two cannot insult me in this manner after the Vedas have spoken!' he roared, but Brahma and Vishnu ignored him.

'Watch me, then!' warned Shiva.

As Brahma and Vishnu watched in astonishment, his body began to glow, his eyes glittered like diamonds and his tangled locks flared out in tongues of flame. Shiva turned into a dazzling column of light. He was brighter than the sun and so tall that the top of the column pierced the sky and vanished into space. The bottom of the column bored deep into the earth and disappeared into the depths of Pataal.

'What is this?' Brahma asked in awe.

'How big is this column?' Vishnu wondered.

Then Shiva's voice echoed down to them, 'I am endless, eternal light. If you think you are greater than me, then discover my beginning and my end!' His thundering laughter shook everything around.

Brahma and Vishnu decided to take up the challenge immediately. They had to find out where the light began under the earth and where it ended beyond the sky. Brahma sent for his pet swan, clambered onto its back and flew away. Vishnu turned himself into a boar, and using his tusks and claws, began to dig into the earth.

Brahma flew higher and higher, past the moon and the stars, and entered outer space, flying beyond the planets and the Milky Way. He asked Surya, the sun god, 'Do you know where this column ends?'

Surya smiled. 'No, Lord Brahma. This column of light goes on and on.'

Vishnu dug through the earth and beneath the ocean, clawing past the netherworld of Pataal, where Yama reigned as king. 'Do you know where this light ends?' asked Vishnu, tired after digging for so long.

Yama laughed and shook his head. 'It goes on forever, way past the horizon.'

After a long while Brahma and Vishnu returned wearily to Swarga. At once the column of light became smaller and smaller until it was just about the size of a normal shivalingam that can be seen in a temple. Vishnu bent down to worship this form of Shiva, but Brahma stood stubbornly to one side. Vishnu looked up at him in surprise.

'I am not going to bow down to Shiva,' said Brahma. 'I have seen the top end of the light. Ask Ketaki; she saw me do so.' He pointed to the Ketaki flower growing in the garden.

Now Ketaki is very pretty but also rather silly. Wanting to please the great god Brahma, she said, 'Oh yes! I saw Lord Brahma touch the end of the light. I was there.'

Shiva had heard enough! He knew Ketaki was lying and he hated lies. A terrible demon called Bhairava darted out of the shivalingam, and everyone cowered when they saw his

enormous fangs and razor-sharp nails. His big saucer-like eyes were red with rage and he swung a shining sword which sliced off one of Brahma's five heads. This made Brahma realize just how much weaker he was than Shiva. He should never have questioned the supreme god of the gods. So Brahma quickly bent down to worship the shivalingam.

Shiva had won the argument, but Bhairava had a problem. He had hurt Brahma, the chief of priests, and that was a sin which had to be punished. Brahma's head stuck to Bhairava's hand and

would not come off, even though Bhairava yanked and pulled and scraped and sawed. So he went on a long pilgrimage and finally reached Varanasi. Here, sitting by the banks of the river Ganga, he prayed for forgiveness and soon the head fell away and vanished under water.

Shiva really is an amazing god. He can become a glowing pillar of pure light and he can also turn himself into a terrible demon. He is beautiful and ugly, kind and terrible, all at the same time!

The Magnificent Archer

Taraka was the king of the asuras. He was a proud creature who thought he could overcome Lord Indra, the powerful commander of Swarga's army. Taraka ranged his demons against the gods and fought a fearsome battle. But of course, the gods were victorious and Taraka was killed by Lord Indra himself.

Taraka left behind three sons—Taraksa, Kamalaksa and Vidyunmalin—who swore to avenge the killing of their father. The brothers knew that special powers were needed to defeat Indra. So, cleverly, they decided to pray to Brahma for a boon. They spent years in fierce meditation, fasting and praying until Brahma was pleased enough to appear before them and ask them what they wanted.

'Honoured Lord of Creation,' Taraksa began. 'Bless us so that we become such powerful warriors that no living creature on land, in the sea or in the air can kill us. And we can live forever.'

Brahma had listened patiently, but now he shook

his head. 'You want to become immortal, and that is a boon I cannot give. Everything on earth has to die some day.'

The brothers looked at each other. 'Suppose you allow us to choose how we'll die?' Kamalaksa asked.

'Yes, that I can do,' agreed Brahma. As he was feeling generous, he added, 'And each of you can ask for a separate boon.'

'Give us each a city to rule,' was Vidyunmalin's request. 'Taraksa's city should be made of gold, Kamalaksa's of silver, and mine of iron.'

'Done!' said Brahma.

Now it was Kamalaksa's turn to make a wish. 'As my boon, I want these cities to be destroyed only by the greatest of the gods. Everyone else should find them impossible to conquer.'

'Granted!' exclaimed Brahma, and thought that the brothers were rather foolish to ask for such simple boons. He had the power to grant them a great deal more.

But then Taraksa said, very softly, 'I wish, lord, that by the boon you grant me, this greatest of the gods will be able to destroy our three cities and kill us all only if he uses just one arrow.'

Brahma sat up immediately. 'What do you mean, one arrow?' He stared in surprise at Taraksa.

'I'll explain, lord. Only one arrow can be used to destroy the three cities and there can be just one try. Otherwise, we three brothers will remain alive forever.'

Brahma frowned. This was getting much more complicated than he had expected. He wished he could go back on his word, but all he could do now was hope that the brothers would behave. 'Well,' he sighed, 'with my blessings, you three have your boons, but do be careful how you use them.'

Did Brahma think the brothers would remain behind long enough to hear his warning? They were off, already plotting and planning their future.

They employed Maya, the architect of the asuras, to build three cities, one of gold, another of silver and the third of iron. And how skilful Maya was! He filled the spaces with beautiful palaces and gardens and kept the three cities aloft in the air to revolve around the earth, like planets. The city of gold's orbit was in upper space, the silver city's in mid-air and the iron city hovered just above the earth. A lake sparkled at the centre of each city, and this lake had magical powers—a quick dip in its waters would heal an asura's battle wounds at once.

Now the brothers were sure they were indestructible. They began to conquer other lands, and their success made them cruel and greedy. There was no peace in heaven or on earth any more. They killed innocent people, attacking hermitages where gentle sages lived, burning their huts and chopping down their forests. Then they declared war on the gods. Indra's mighty army was defeated because the brothers were protected by Brahma's boon, and their injured soldiers had merely to bathe in the magical lakes to be fighting fit again.

Indra was very angry with Brahma. How irresponsible could he get? Soon the demons would overrun Swarga, and then what would Brahma do? Indra marched up to the

white-haired god and said, 'Lord Brahma, do something and do it now!'

Brahma thought for a long time, and then he said, 'We need a brilliant archer, someone who can pierce the three revolving cities with one arrow.'

'Shiva?'

'Of course! He is the supreme archer and his giant bow Pinaka is so big that it can make any arrow fly through the air like a bolt of lightning. Only he can save us.'

Indra rushed to Mount Kailash and fell at Shiva's

feet. Not far away, all the gods of heaven waited anxiously.

'Please, please, great god of destruction,' said Indra, 'only you can defeat and kill the three evil demons.'

Shiva looked at Indra in surprise. 'Why do you say that?' he asked.

'Because you have the powerful Pinaka.'

'What makes you think I have the strength to pierce three cities at

once?' Shiva asked doubtfully. 'These cities are not ordinary cities, you know...'

The other gods interrupted, 'We will all lend you our strength and make you so strong that the arrow you use will burn everything that comes in its way.'

They asked for the divine architect Vishwakarma's help and he created a giant chariot that would be pulled by the

seven white horses of the sun god Surya. Gods can do wonderful things with yoga, and now they used their knowledge to send all their strength to Shiva, making him supremely powerful. He again became Mahadev, the greatest of the gods.

'I need a master charioteer,' said Shiva, 'to drive the horses swiftly across the earth and the sky.'

Brahma himself picked up the reins of the chariot. Shiva blazed forth from Swarga, followed by the divine army. Indra, who controlled the skies, parted the clouds to provide a clear path. The Maruts—the wind gods—blew on the chariot's wheels, and Kubera, the god of wealth, sounded his conch. Its call threw a challenge to the asuras—the gods were ready to fight!

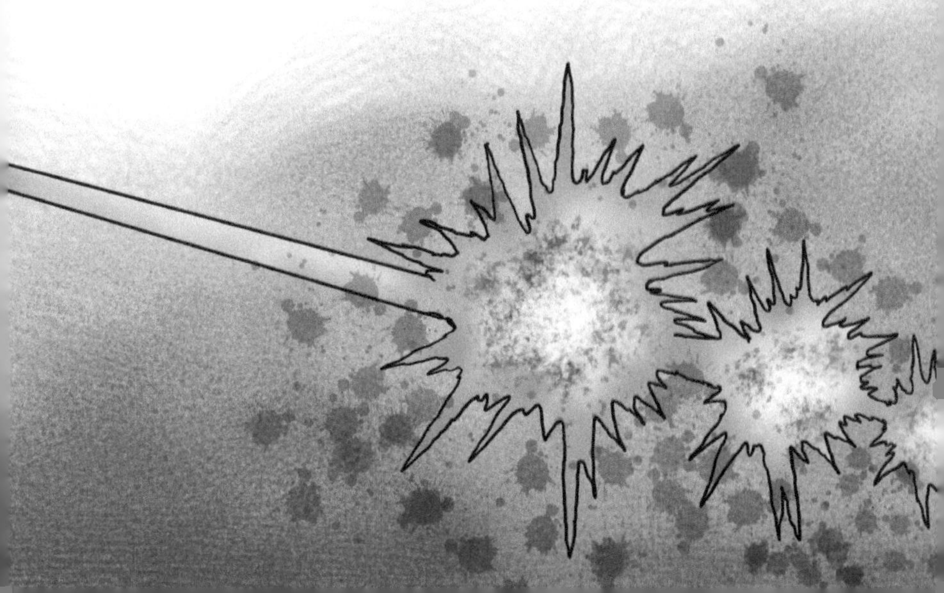

Taraksa, Kamalaksa and Vidyunmalin emerged with their armies from the gold, silver and iron cities, and the battle began. The sky went dark with arrows flying in all directions. The demons, pushed back into their cities by the gods, hid behind the high walls and showered the army of Swarga with spears and balls of fire.

Meanwhile, Brahma guided Shiva's chariot far up into outer space until they could look down and see the three cities revolving below them. Shiva fitted Pinaka with a huge arrow, its tip flashing like fire. Then he waited patiently.

Suddenly, for just a short moment, the three cities fell into a straight line below him as they orbited the earth. Shiva aimed downwards and let the arrow fly. It went cleanly through all three cities and they were burnt to ashes. Everyone in the cities, including the kings Taraksa, Kamalaksa and Vidyunmalin, was killed instantly in the enormous flames.

A triumphant Shiva returned to Swarga at the head of Indra's army. Everyone gathered round to shower him with flowers and sing the praises of Shiva-Pinaki, the champion archer of the universe.

www.ingramcontent.com/pod-product-compliance
Lightning Source LLC
Chambersburg PA
CBHW030336310726
48979CB00001B/54

* 9 7 8 8 1 2 9 1 4 5 1 4 7 *